A SURGEON GOT ME

LUCA

JUST BAE

ISBN: 978-1-925988-51-2

CONTENTS

CHAPTER ONE

Doctor Luca Michaelson hears his pager going off nonstop.

"We have a twelve-car pileup, about fifteen minutes out! Multiple traumas, so we need all hands on deck!" Luca hears from out in the hospital's hallway.

Luca groans; Holly's voice ringing in his ears a bit too loudly. It looks like it's going to be one of those nights and he's definitely too tired.

Once the surgeon's fully up, feeling a bit groggy, Luca hops off the bottom bunk and grapples for his pager in the dark.

Before he can even touch the floor, the door opens and in comes angry-looking Nurse Amber.

"Michaelson, we've been paging you for the last ten minutes! Get your ass to ER now!"

Not a second later, she's gone, probably off to scream at the other group.

There are many things that Luca enjoys about his job, and Amber's yelling isn't one of them - especially when she's in one of her moods in the wee-hours of the morning. Luca hated being on the receiving end of her tirade.

Two minutes later, Luca is up, running out of the door and down the hall to the ER. His white coat billowing behind him as he hurries.

* * *

Being the highest ranked trauma center in the state, Mornington Hospital's ER is constantly busy. Car crashes are an everyday occurrence, along with other traumas that never seem to conclude. The ways people injure themselves is astounding.

Luca reached the ambulance loading dock and is immediately handed a surgical gown and a pair of rubber gloves. Nurse Amber scoffs when she sees his rumpled scrubs and bedhead.

"Nice nap?"

Luca rolls his eyes and smirks. "Perfect, actually. Four surgeries in a day will tire you out, not that you would know."

Amber's facial expression turned sour as she turns away huffing. Luca sees Thomas and Holly trying to hide their laughter.

Contrary to this situation, Luca actually gets along with his coworkers. Thomas, who's inside with him, is the most hilarious pediatric surgeon at the hospital. Holly, who usually keeps to herself, is good at dishing out orders in any stressful situation. Luca definitely hands it to her; she's one of the best trauma surgeons he's met.

Despite Amber's tough character, she can be nice sometimes. She has a drive for competitiveness, something she and Luca share in common. Amber was used to being called the best at everything but was in for a wakeup call when she began working with Luca. In actuality, they're a lot more alike than Luca would care to admit. This makes good entertainment when they're battling over the number of surgeries they performed per day.

Just when Luca is tuning back to Thomas instructing Holly about the details of their incoming trauma victims, someone stumbles through the doors and skids to stop of the ambulance bay.

"Hey! Did I miss the party?"

Luca groans seeing Damien grinning while putting on a pair of gloves. He opens his mouth to tell him off before the doors open once again, interrupting.

"Now is not the time for jokes, Dr. Brady."

Subconsciously, everyone straightens up and turns their attention towards Chief Mackwood. She's flanked by both Dr. Armstrong and Dr. Taggart. The expressions on their faces are serious.

* * *

The group are in their final year of residency and haven't been Dr. Mackwood's interns for some time now. Still, they tend to worship the ground she walks on. The novelty of being mentored by one of the best heart surgeons in the country always brought thrills.

A siren blaring close by snaps Holly back to attention. Her expression shifts as she puts on her game face for telling everyone of the situation they will have on their hands.

"Multiple in critical, and a high number of head injuries."

They're in for a long night.

The first ambulance comes screeching to a halt and everyone rushes forward. The next few minutes are a blur of shouted orders and gurneys being wheeled through the ER with moaning patients. Luca follows Thomas into a trauma room to help assess a young girl with a nasty gash on the side of her head.

Luca takes out his flashlight to shine it into the young girl's eyes as Thomas tends to her other injuries. "Hi sweetie, my name is Dr. Michaelson, can you could tell me your name?"

The girl tries to moan out her name but it's obvious she's not conscious enough to articulate well. "Okay, I know it hurts. It's just very important that you try and follow my finger." He waves it in front of her face and is happy to see she can follow the movement perfectly with her half-lidded eyes.

Before Luca can speak, Thomas pipes up, "She's stable for now. I'll take her up for a head CT and page you if she needs surgery. Go help the others."

Luca nods and dashes out and back into the ambulance bay. The last ambulance has just pulled up and Amber is helping the EMTs unload the gurney. He saunters over as vitals are listed.

Luca begins pulling the gurney as Amber spots him and grabs ahold of the end of it. "This patient is mine, I was here first," she growls and Luca sighs.

"There are signs of mild cardiac distress and this patient obviously has a massive head injury, so if you don't mind, this one is mine."

Amber was about to say something when someone clears their throat from behind. The person in question jumps down from the back of the ambulance and Luca freezes.

The woman is young and looks close to Luca's age. Her hair is brunette with curls near the back of her neck. Her eyes are brown and are framed by black-titanium frames. Luca sees there's a large amount of blood on her shirt around the area where it's rolled up. This woman's attractive in a nerdy way. Luca's breath hitches as he watches her twirl her hair nervously.

"If you wouldn't mind, I'd like to assist?"

Luca is so dumbfounded by how cute the woman before him is, that he doesn't realize he's being spoken to. At his look, the woman giggles and twirls her hair again as she starts to push the gurney into the ER, while Luca and Amber trail behind her.

"I was driving to work when I came across the accident. I'm also a trauma surgeon."

It's been too long since Luca has spoken and Amber is starting to look at him out of the corner of her eye. "This isn't normal," she wonders. "Luca Michaelson does not get turned on around women in the ER and is speechless over this one he met not two minutes ago."

Luca comes back to himself when he sees the nurses lifting the patient onto the table while the female trauma surgeon puts on a pair of gloves and gown. His eyes drift over to the patient seeing him trached with a straw. This is Luca's first time seeing this.

"You trached him? With a straw?" The brunette looks up from her assessment of the patient's throat and smiles as her face turns reddish.

"He was going to die. I had no other choice."

Luca shakes his head and smiles as he begins his assessment of the patient's head. Just as he's about to open his mouth to flirt with the trauma surgeon, Amber's pager buzzes.

She reads the page and chuckles. "Holly needs an extra pair of hands in the OR, preferably another trauma surgeon with more experience. You up for it doctor?"

The brunette looks up and smiles. "I'm Dr. Winstead. And I'd love to help if you guys don't mind."

"Come with me." Amber drags Dr. Winstead off and down the hallway while Luca is left alone with the patient. Luca makes sure the patient is stable and sends him off for a CT before seeking out Dr.

Winstead to ask for her first name. Maybe she'll want to go for a drink later.

"Michaelson! There's a stopped heart in OR five!"

Luca huffs and glances toward the hallway Amber and Dr. Winstead just went down before turning and running towards OR five.

He hopes the brunette's patient surgery lasts as long as his.

CHAPTER TWO

Several hours later, Luca is dragging along as he comes out of the OR; his scrub cap hanging loosely from his hand.

The surgery had not gone well. Amidst complication after complication, the patient's heart had survived, but would possibly have repercussions on his everyday health.

Luca turned the corner to find his coworkers sitting around the nurse's station exhausted. Damien was snoring with his head in his arms and Holly was slumped against the wall. Even Amber looked ready to sleep for about a week. The only one who looked awake was Thomas, and he was going over charts smiling.

Luca doesn't know why Thomas is always in a

good mood.

Amber perked up at the sight of Thomas and grins. "You just missed the cute trauma surgeon."

Luca straightened up at the mention of Dr. Winstead realizing whom Amber's referring to. He groans sagging in his chair. If Luca could, he'd bang his head against the desk nonstop.

Damien groggily looks around. "What'd I miss?"

Amber starts giggling. "Michaelson here has a crush on the trauma surgeon that trached the patient with a straw."

Holly sits up at thinking of the brunette who helped her earlier in the OR.

"Come on man, can't you go a week without wanting to get into some nurse's panties?" Damien says as he rubs his goatee.

Luca rolls his eyes. "First of all," he starts. "I don't have a crush on anyone. Aren't we on the clock here?" Then he turns to Damien, "And I can't help it if the ladies are constantly around willing to have some fun."

Everyone yells, "Oooooooo!"

Luca smiles and stands up. "Anyway, my shift is officially over. See you all tomorrow bright and early."

Luca walks out of the hallway to a chorus of intakes' groans.

CHAPTER THREE

Luca Michaelson has a problem.

He doesn't commit after hookups, learning in medical school when his first fling, Alice Walker told him they were free to see anyone, at the beginning of their rendezvous. However, Luca had at first perceived them as the perfect couple. Since then, Luca has never settled down. It's easier that way. Just sex is nice and it's better that he chose a career where it's hard to get emotionally involved.

It's been a week since the night of the twelve-car pileup and Luca is still thinking about Dr. Winstead. No matter what he does, he cannot get her out of his head. Luca, when he sees a patient's family member trailing the gurney with blood-spattered clothes, pictures Dr. Winstead's clothes that night, too. Then, he'll see someone sipping from a straw and think about how the brunette trached a patient with one. And if Luca sees a woman with black-rimmed glasses, all he can think about is the brunette's eyes and her nerdy look.

Luca begins to believe he's going mad.

He's been at the bar across the street from the hospital more times in the past week than he's been in the last year. Every night ends the same: he goes, he gets drunk, he starts looking for a hookup, and then he leaves because he starts thinking about Dr. Winstead.

The surgeon can't stop imagining running his hands down Dr. Winstead's curvy figure.

"Luca!"

A shout startles him from his daydream, making him spill his charts on the floor in the process. He glares at Damien as the plastic surgeon laughs and walks by. Luca is a mess and it's been like this all week. To him, it's Dr. Winstead's fault. Dr. Winstead, who he was only in the presence of for five minutes, and spoke all of six words to.

As Luca hastily picking up his charts, he sees Holly crouch down and begins to help. "So," she starts, "you ready for the merger with the hospital down the road?"

Luca groans. "Not really," he blurts. "We don't need any more traffic around here. Especially when Amber is running things. It wouldn't surprise me if I had to clip an aneurysm of hers by the end of the week."

Holly chuckles as they stand back up and she hands him the rest of his charts. Her eyebrows scrunch as she debates on what to say to Luca next. "About that surgeon from last week?"

"Seriously, you're still on that? Yeah, she looked good, that's it. No biggie," Luca huffs and turns before Holly can figure out the trauma surgeon is all he's been thinking about all week.

* * *

The remainder of the day moves slowly. Luca has back-to-back surgeries up until five in the evening. When he finally leaves the OR, he finds the hallways in utter chaos. Most of the faces Luca has never seen before, and he realizes it's because the employees from the hospital down the road have begun to arrive.

Thomas whizzes past him; his bloodied shoes leaving a trail behind. When he sees Luca, he pauses looking at him crazily. "Michaelson, trauma needs you in OR one stat!" Thomas yells before dashing off.

Luca sighs before taking off running. Looks like yet another long night is in store for all.

Luca reaches the OR and immediately begins the scrubbing process. He vaguely makes out someone gowning a surgeon in the OR in front of him, but the woman doesn't look like Holly.

When he finishes scrubbing, he rushes to the door and goes in. "You paged?" Luca asks as a surgical nurse helps him put his gown on.

"Yeah, I've got a patient with a bad spinal injury and could use a consult before I go in to repair it."

Luca whips his head around at the voice and promptly loses his mind. It's Dr. Winstead standing in front of him once again.

He knows why she's here. There was talk that she worked for the hospital down the road. Now with the merger, she'll be working at Mornington with Luca.

Luca takes a moment to inhale before smiling at the trauma surgeon. He walks forward to see the x-rays. Dr. Winstead smiles, almost as if she's nervous. "The patient fell out of a second-story window and it doesn't look too good at the moment."

She hands the x-rays to Luca as the nurses and anesthesiologist prep the patient to go under. Luca observes the scans and lets out a low whistle. "Yeah, this is bad. We're going to need to go in and do a spinal repair right away."

Dr. Winstead lets out a sigh, disappointed at the patient's prognosis. "Well, you can take it from here. This is above my usual patient level," she replies as she begins to discard her gown and gloves. Quickly, Luca makes a decision.

"Wait!"

Dr. Winstead is startled and looks up. Luca clears his throat as his face beams. "Please stay. I mean, if you're not busy, please observe, even help." Luca giggles and comes back to himself. "You can watch the magician perform his magic," Luca wiggles his fingers towards Dr. Winstead.

Dr. Winstead nods looking embarrassed before she wrings her hands nervously and gestures for Luca to begin. Luca grins and then goes about preparing for the surgery.

"So," he starts, drawing out the end of the word, "what's your name?"

Dr. Winstead laughs a little while raising her eyebrow. "Hmm, Dr. Winstead?" she says it like it's a question.

Luca shakes his head. "I mean your first name. As nice as it's been to call you Dr. Winstead in my head all week, I'd like to know your first name."

The brunette sputters and becomes flustered at the fact that Luca is thinking about her.

"Bethany," she says quietly blushing. Luca wonders if her reactions spread to her bosom. He finds himself imagining pulling up Bethany's shirt and finding out for himself.

Luca shakes the thought out his head. "Scalpel," he says and is handed the instrument by one of the attending nurses. He smirks as he cuts into his patient. "Bethany, it's nice to meet you. I'm Dr. Luca Michaelson."

"I know," Bethany replies quickly, and then her eyes widen as she backtracks. "I mean, I heard—from your coworkers. Last week, I asked the other trauma surgeon for your name. Not for any reason, I mean, I just forgot to ask you myself before I left and it seemed impolite. You know?" Bethany takes a deep breath and shakes her head. "And I'm going to stop rambling and embarrassing myself any further."

Luca chuckles and wasn't the only one appreciating the moment. "I don't mind. I actually find it cute." He sends another smirk Bethany's way as he continues to work on his patient. The more Luca flirts, the more open Bethany becomes. It's fun to watch.

"Cute? Well, thanks," Bethany says, almost like she had to force herself to say it.

They continue to talk for the next half hour and Luca even brings up the straw trach. Bethany blushes under the praise and brushes off Luca's compliments. Luca sees that anytime Bethany's complimented, she says they aren't true and brushes them off causing him to quickly counter.

Soon enough, Bethany gets paged for a consultation down in the ER. She looks disappointed she has to leave and walks toward the exit slowly.

"Hey, Bethany?"

"Yes?"

Luca smiles and pauses for a second. "Want to go out for coffee or something like that? Let's say tomorrow?"

Bethany smiles and nods. "I'm off at six. I'll wait around for you to finish your shift."

"Great. See you then, Beth."

Bethany's face reddens at the nickname.

"Damn it, damn it, damn it!"

It's half past six the next day and Luca's in a bit of trouble in the OR.

Holly has her hands in the patient's open chest cavity as Luca frantically thinks about what to do next.

This surgery had been rocky from the start. The patient crashed three times before he was even put on the operating table and was currently cardiac-arresting for the fourth time. To any surgeon other than Luca, the patient would have been a lost cause, but Holly and Luca were not going down without a fight.

Truth be told, Holly was Luca's favorite to assist in surgeries. Her skills and quickness were incomparable. She was as dedicated to her patients like him, and together they made one hell of a team.

It was another ten minutes before Holly gave a low sigh and slowly retracted her bloodied hands from the patient's chest as the heart monitor continued to flatline. Her voice was grim when she called, "Time of death: 6:34."

Luca ripped off his gloves and scrub cap. "Damn it," says Luca as he quickly wrestles out of his surgical gown.

"Luca?" Holly calls as he washes his arms in the scrub sink.

He sighs. "I know this patient was a lost cause, but it doesn't make losing him any easier." Holly nods as Luca frantically scrubs his hands and arms in the sink. "And I was supposed to meet Bethany half an hour ago. Now, she's probably going to hate me. This was our first date or at least attempt at one."

"Luca, please stop!"

He pauses and looks down finding his arms looking red. The scrubber falls into the sink as he groans. "Look, I'm sure she'll understand. She's a surgeon too, so she knows what it's like. I'll take it from here, inform the family, and you hurry up. Don't worry. I got this."

Luca wipes his forehead and Holly smiles like that's all he needed to hear.

Ten minutes later, Luca's running down towards the main entrance to find Bethany leaning against the wall, tapping away at her phone. She's dressed in a grey cardigan and fitted jeans, with her thick-rimmed glasses sliding off her nose. She looks so relaxed, and Luca just wants to skip coffee, lay down next to her and fall asleep.

Luca makes his way towards her while excuses are already popping up in his head. When Bethany looks up, she sees Luca in front of her, babbling nervously. "I'm so sorry. I got caught up in surgery and thought I'd be finished early. The shit was a pain in the ass and unfortunately, we couldn't end up saving him—"

"Luca, it's okay! Are you okay?" Bethany looks at him in concern, but her eyes are twinkling. "I understand. Surgeon here, remember?" She points to herself with an eyebrow raised.

"Yeah, I'll be fine." Luca lets out a breath he wasn't even aware he was holding. He's never been so concerned with reassuring someone like this before.

It's foreign and makes him feel slightly uneasy but grateful at the same time.

Bethany hesitated before asking her next question. "You said you lost the patient?" Luca nods. "Well, would you like to ditch the coffee and come over to my place? You need some cheering up to do."

Observing Luca's shocked facial expression, Bethany blushes to realize what it sounds like she's offering. "I meant, you could come over and we could order a pizza and watch Netflix or something. I know when I lose a patient I always just want to stay in and avoid people for that evening. Not that I didn't want to have coffee with you! You know what I mean—"

Luca cuts her off by grabbing her hand and Bethany's mouth snaps shut. Luca smiles as he squeezes her soft hand. "Pizza sounds good," Luca says gesturing for Bethany to lead the way.

Luca has no idea what he's doing.

The word 'date' isn't really in his vocabulary. Sure, he's taken a girl out for a drink or two before ultimately taking them back to his apartment, but they hardly counted as dates. His one-night-stands were always like ghosts that come at night and go in the morning. Luca made sure they understood his 'casual-hookup' stance.

Besides, Luca has never felt the urge to look for something more. While most he knows outside of work are settling down by getting married and having children, Luca doesn't see the point especially being twenty-nine at the door knocking on thirty. His appearance deceives many as if he's in his early twenties. Luca intends to use that to his advantage as much as possible.

It's not like being a surgeon offers him much leeway anyway. Even if Luca wanted to date, he works about seventy hours a week, so it's not like he even has the time. The only potential candidates in his dating pool that would understand would come from a similar medical background. And there's no way he'd ever think about dating any of his coworkers.

Bethany is his coworker now though. And Luca doesn't understand how he's only known this woman for two short days and already feels more for her than any of the women in his life.

They're lounging on Bethany's sofa, binge-watching a trashy reality show. An empty pizza box sits on the coffee table along with two half-empty beer cans and Bethany's rambling on about the most complicated surgery she's ever had to perform while Luca can't stop staring.

His chest feels light and there's this feeling he's having. Every time Bethany smiles, his heart trips over itself before going in overdrive. The heat radiating off of Bethany's side is driving Luca crazy, and all he wants to do is move over until there's no space left between. Bethany's thigh has been pressing all along him all evening. There's a tingling sensation in Luca's fingers, almost as if he's aching to reach out and twine his fingers with Bethany's. He has his suspicions on what's happening, but would rather not examine it too closely.

"And then, get this, just as we're closing up, the patient flatlines again and—"

Luca laughs awkwardly realizing Bethany wasn't joking about her patient. Though, it was as if Luca had just joined the conversation.

Bethany stops abruptly and looks at him. "Is there something wrong?" Luca stops laughing and shakes his head. He doesn't want to let Bethany know he's currently having a panicking attack.

Bethany worries for a second before moving closer. Her side is now a body of heat, pressed tightly against Luca's. She holds his hand to calm him down. Without saying another word, she focuses back on the TV and resumes watching.

Maybe it's a date.

Surprisingly, the night ends with Bethany walking Luca to the door.

They had just topped off the evening trading surgery horror stories and getting to know one another. Luca had flirted with Bethany the entire night, her eventually warming up and flirting back was just as aggressively. It was the first time Luca had ever spent a night with a woman he was attracted to and didn't at least end up making out with her. Truth be told, it was the most fun he had had in months.

Now, Bethany is leaning against the opening of her apartment door, the gold numbers of 303 glintings in the low hallway light. Luca is hesitant to leave and doesn't want the night to end. He's scared that once he's alone, he'll go back to his old ways.

"So," Luca says as he shoves his hands in his pockets.

The right side of Bethany's mouth pulls up a bit. "So—" she repeats back, drawing out the end of the word. She takes a small breath before beginning, "We could do this—"

"Let me take you out to dinner," Luca blurts out without a second thought. He doesn't know why he even said it; he's never actually gone on a dinner date with a woman before.

"Sounds perfect." Her smile graces her features.

A second later, Bethany moves over and plants a small kiss on Luca's cheek. It happened so fast that Luca isn't even sure if he imagined it or not.

There's a wicked gleam in Bethany's eye as she backs into her apartment and holds the door. "See you later, Dr. Michaelson." She quickly shuts it and Luca is left standing out in the hallway dumfounded.

A shiver runs through his body as he goes over Bethany's tone of voice when calling him by his professional name. He finds that he likes it quite a bit.

Luca smiles and turns to walk down the corridor.

Nobody has to know if there's a slight skip in his step until he reaches the street.

CHAPTER FIVE

Luca and Bethany have texted each other at all hours.

Bethany is usually the one to text first since she enjoys taking the earlier shifts at the hospital.

"Good morning!"

"How are you this cheerful so early in the morning?"

"I've been in surgery since 5 am."

"Why are you talking to me then? Go rest."

"Ok, but I have coffee waiting for you. Would you rather I drink it?"

"You're a godsend! Be there in 15."

Luca, more often than not, attempts to send dirty texts during his lunch break if they aren't working on the same shift.

"What are you wearing?

"I'm not doing this with you. I have on my scrubs and a white jacket. Nothing new to report, LOL."

"Oh come on, Beth."

"Whining will get you nowhere."

"You're no fun."

A large portion of their text conversations also consists of complaining about their current patients.

"This mother of four is an absolute pain in the ass. I've had to explain a thoracotomy at least five times already."

"Yikes. I have an inoperable tumor and the patient refuses to accept my prognosis."

"Please kill me. My patient is refusing treatment even though they're going to die."

"Just had to clean up puke for almost a half an hour."

Luca doesn't care when his friends tease him for always being glued to his phone.

A week later finds Luca sitting behind the nurse's station and drowning in charts. The slap of more paperwork snaps him out of his thoughts. He looks up to find Damien leaning against the station with a cocky grin. Luca sighs, his headache is already coming on.

"So—" Damien starts as he opens one of his charts, "Did you sleep with the new trauma surgeon yet?" The guy even wiggles his eyebrows.

Luca doesn't want Damien to know he and Beth haven't slept together yet. Over the past week, they've gone out a few times but Beth acts nervously whenever Luca suggests they move onto more fun activities at home. Bethany laughs and tries to change the subject as quickly as possible.

Luca doesn't know what he's doing wrong, and frankly, he's going insane from not having been laid in a while. Bethany and her perfection are killing him.

The silence stretches on for a few seconds as Luca tries to avoid answering the question. When he doesn't reply, Damien raises his eyebrows. "No way dude, you didn't—"

Damien's comment is cut off by an array of shouts and footsteps pounding in from the ambulance bay. A second later, Holly is seen pushing a gurney rushing down the hallway. Bethany is straddling a patient that's unconscious and is doing chest compressions as the patient's pushed straight to the operating room. Her white coat is covered with blood and her glasses are down to the end of her nose.

"He's crashing! We need to get to OR, stat! We need cardio!"

The whole scene is over in less than a minute. The image of Bethany straddling the patient, her thighs framing their thin frame, is replaying inside Luca's head. He wants to run his hands through her hair, maybe hold it from behind. *Maybe Bethany has a kink for that?* Luca sees Beth as shy in person and kinky when turned up.

"Man, you are so whipped!"

Luca hears Damien close to his ear. "I'm not whipped," he grumbles as he starts shuffling through the charts. "We're not going out."

Damien smiles. "I cannot believe you two haven't slept together yet. How does it feel to be the one working so hard to get laid, dude?"

The pen in Luca's hand makes a sizable indent in the chart from how hard he's gripping it. Damien doesn't notice his shift in mood and continues to go in. "Seriously. Even lame man Thomas is getting some from that new badass ortho surgeon Becky."

Luca is saved by his pager going off. He smiles and waves the object in Damien's face. "Sorry. I've got a craniotomy coming in. Have fun with your rhinoplasties buddy!"

CHAPTER SIX

Luca hasn't been laid in a month, which is something he hasn't had to endure since high school. He was new in this town and even he had women at the bar across the street who gushed over him. Lately, he's gotten cold feet to even take one of them home if offered a chance mainly because of Bethany's face keeps flashing in his mind.

Two hours later, Luca is exhausted headed to the on-call room. His last surgery had left him drained and he still has about five hours left on his shift.

When he opens the door, light floods into the shadowed room and illuminates the bunk on the far wall. Luca's throat goes dry when he sees Bethany sit up squinting against the light.

"Oh. I didn't know you were in here." Luca goes

to close the door when Bethany yawns. She lays back down, her scrubs wrinkling further as she gets comfortable again. Smiling at Luca, she pats the open space next to her as an invitation.

Not one to turn down an opportunity, Luca slides in. They're laying on their backs, shoulder to shoulder, and Luca can't get enough of the heat radiating off of Bethany's body.

For a few minutes, the sound of their breaths and Luca's racing heart could be heard in the silent room.

"How was your day?"

Luca almost laughs.

Bethany chuckles and starts rambling on about her multiple surgeries and traumas. Luca can't help but stare as she gestures wildly with her hands and recounts every little detail. Bethany's eyes are twinkling as she explains a complicated operation she had to endure with Holly.

Luca's so captivated by Bethany's tale that he doesn't realize what he's doing; his hands tangle into Bethany's hair and he's tugging her forward to press his lips against hers.

Luca feels Bethany gasp. Suddenly, her hands wrapped around Luca's neck and pulling him closer. The kiss turns frantic quickly.

They stay like that; trading kisses for what feels

like minutes, hours and years. Luca can't tell, but he doesn't ever want to stop.

All too fast Bethany pulls away. Luca's vision blurs for a minute and then he refocuses in on Bethany looking at him. "What was that for?" Bethany sounds breathless and shocked.

"You're cute when you ramble," Luca grins watching Bethany blush. "Honestly? I've wanted to do that since I saw you jump out of that ambulance."

Bethany yanks Luca back in. This time, there's nothing gentle about their kissing. Bethany bites at Luca's lips, almost enough to be painful. Luca's tongue quickly becomes well accustomed to Bethany's as his hands roam all down her back.

Before Luca knows it, Bethany has him pinned to the bed, her thighs straddling his waist. Luca's mind flashes to the scene from earlier with Bethany giving chest compressions to the patient below her. He chuckles but is cut off as a tongue laves its way over the side of his neck. Seconds later, Bethany's teeth are nipping and sucking their way to his collarbone. Luca doesn't think he's ever been this turned on.

"I've wanted—" Bethany kisses against the underside of Luca's jaw, "to do this—" then a kiss to his Adam's apple, "for weeks," she finishes with a kiss to his collarbone. Luca moans when Bethany gazes into his eyes. He feels the intensity going straight to his groin.

"Then why haven't you said anything?"

Bethany just shrugs and suddenly looks shy again. "I wasn't sure if you wanted this."

Luca laughs and flips Bethany over so he's the one on top of her. "Are you kidding me?" He grabs Bethany's wrists and pins them above her head. "I took you out! I even had to endure Damien telling me how 'whipped' I am over you," he punctuates each word with a kiss down Bethany's neck.

Bethany giggles and leans up to capture Luca's lips again. They kiss for a few more minutes and Luca's just beginning to trail his hands down Bethany's body before she protests and rolls out from under him.

"No, I'm not having sex with you in a break room, Mr. Michaelson."

"Oh come on," his whine is raspy. "I've been a good boy for far too long. Now it's about time for me to do something bad."

Bethany laughs and rolls her eyes. Just as she's about to ponder the thought, her pager goes off. It's her cue so she gets up, gathers herself and walks towards the door. "See you later, Dr. Luca."

Luca silently wills his manhood to go back down.

Two days later and they still haven't done *anything*.

Luca is convinced that Bethany is doing this to drive him crazy.

Maybe she's conspiring with Holly. The two trauma surgeons have become close and formed a team of sorts. When they're not performing surgeries together, Holly is joining them at their lunch table or butting into their conversations. She seems to take great joy in Luca's frustration and Luca doesn't find it amusing.

They're all sitting around a table in the hospital cafeteria and Bethany is telling the story of her first solo surgery. Luca's hand slowly inches its way up to Bethany's thigh. Bethany is so absorbed in spinning the tale for Holly that she isn't even aware of what Luca is doing.

Luca grumbles and tightens his grip.

Bethany startles a little and looks in his direction. Luca smiles innocently and playfully blows a kiss without Holly noticing. Holly sighs and gets up when she feels her pager going off.

Luca comes over and sits next to her wanting to kiss but Bethany slowly pulls away. "Luca," she rebukes. "We're at work."

Luca smiles while his hand wanders a little higher on Bethany's thigh and brushes against the clit area. This time, her breath hitches and her bottom lip slips in between her teeth. Luca finds the sight amazing. "So?" he breathes into Bethany's ear.

Bethany shakes herself out of her stupor and pulls back to look at Luca again. Her expressions shifts and she glances around before dropping her voice to almost a whisper. "We can't do this here. You should come over tonight."

"Hmm, so you're inviting me to your place for what reason?"

"Do you want me to spoil the surprise?"

Luca can't do anything but swallow and shake his head. At that, Bethany smiles and entwines her fingers with Luca's hand. She stands and pulls Luca towards the exit, all the while keeping a firm grip on his hand. "Come on, let's go watch that cardiac procedure Amber was rambling about earlier."

For the next hour, Luca is paying close attention to Bethany's hand resting nicely in his. He can't help but think that their hands fit pretty well together.

Luca sees that Bethany is a tease.

Every few minutes, the brunette trauma surgeon leans over to whisper something in Luca's ear and all the neurosurgeon can focus on is her warm breath ghosting over the shell of his ear. Bethany's thumb is rubbing patterns into Luca's hand, and he doesn't think he can remember one second of the surgery Amber is performing.

CHAPTER SEVEN

Their shifts are finally over and Bethany is trying to open the door to her apartment but is failing quite spectacularly with Luca's arms wrapped around her from behind as she's being sucked on the neck.

There's a dangerous feeling spreading throughout his body as he strokes his hand through Bethany's hair. He's never felt like this; this pure adoration is completely foreign. Yet, Bethany still doesn't cave into his wishes and after an hour of foreplay and dinner, Dr. Michaelson is once again out the door.

It's been going on a month now and Luca is wondering where he and Beth are going in this relationship. They never had a deep conversation, but Luca is sure it's not just a fling. Yet, he often wonders, *"Are we serious? Or just friends with limited benefits?"* Luca isn't sleeping with anyone and he's almost sure Bethany isn't either. They spend every minute if they're not in the operating room with each other.

For the first time, Luca finds himself wanting to settle down. He would like to show Bethany off to his family. It would be nice if he could come home to her, eat dinner and spend the night.

Surprisingly one day, Luca is willing to ask his co-worker, Thomas for advice. For once in life, he didn't want to fuck this up.

The moment he does, he's in an empty hospital hallway being grilled by Damien and Amber, while Thomas' sitting off to the side.

"Is she good in bed?"

"Have you scored yet dude?"

"Sickos, if you don't mind, I came here to talk to Thomas, not to be interrogated."

Amber puts her hand over her mouth, while Damien looks like he's going to continue pressing.

Thomas sees what's about to happen and comes to the rescue. "What's up, Luca?"

Luca slumps back against the wall and scrubs a

hand across his face. "I don't know what to do about the nurse."

"Who, Bethany?"

"Yeah, who else would I be talking about?"

"My bad, dude. What's up?"

"I like her and have never felt like this over a girl before. I'm almost thirty and I feel like if I don't do something soon then—"

Amber hears Luca and comes over to put her hands on his shoulders. Luca didn't even realize he was hyperventilating. "Calm down."

"Have you gone on a date with her?"

Luca nods.

"Okay. Have you done other things?"

Luca nods again.

Damien yells. "Okay Mr. I-don't-do-girlfriends, she's your girlfriend. What's the problem?"

"She's not my girlfriend!" Luca yells, flinging his arms out. "Sure, we've slept together and gone on some dates, but she's not my girlfriend!"

Thomas' eyes go wide as Bethany comes out of a room nearby and just stands there. Her demeanor spells disappointment and Luca's stomach drops to his feet.

"Damn, she heard me!" is all he thinks at the moment

"Is that all I am to you?" Bethany's voice is low and cracking. "Just some fuck? A toy to have fun with?" A bitter laugh escapes her mouth as she reaches for her glasses.

Luca can barely breathe. "Bethany, listen—"

"No!" The word is so sharp Luca stumbles back. "I don't want to hear it! Whatever this was, which I had the wrong idea about, is over."

Luca reaches out for Bethany's hand and she backs up. "Don't touch me! You liar!" She dashes off with tears streaming down her cheeks.

"No, Beth," Luca mumbles as he backs up until his back hits the wall and buries his face in his hands. He can't hear Amber, Damien Thomas calling his name.

None of it matters. Bethany's gone and it's his fault.

A week passes and Luca avoids the on-call room at all costs. He tries to schedule his shifts so they don't coincide with Bethany's and tries to avoid all conversations outside of work.

Amber has had it with his moping and has tried to convince Luca to talk to Bethany. Every time she does, she receives the same response: "She asked me not to talk to her, so I'm respecting her wishes. I don't need her."

Luca misses the warmth of Bethany's palm in his and her quiet laughter that she always tried to muffle into his neck. He misses the kisses Bethany would press to on side of his neck for their dinner dates. He even misses the 'no sex in the on-call room' rule because it meant she respected herself.

So, Luca goes through the motions. He goes to work, performs his duties, saves lives, and tries not to get in anyone's way, especially Bethany's. More often than not, he ends up at night at the bar across the street after work before calling an Uber to take him home. He hates being home alone. Bethany's silence is closing in and suffocating him.

Luca's bed feels hard and cold, devoid of the warmth and sweat that usually occupied the sheets when he dreamt about Bethany. The mattress seems far too large; an empty space adding to the feeling of remorse.

He's never been so wrecked over someone, not even his cat when it had run away.

***

Back in the OR the next morning, Luca's reeling from his thoughts. He shakes his head and tries to refocus on the patient lying on the operating table. The lights are too bright and his hands are too unsteady.

"Dr. Michaelson?" Thomas calls Luca in his professional doctor's voice. Luca looks up to find him peering over his mask, his scalpel frozen in midair. "You okay?"

Luca clears his throat and rolls his shoulders backward. There's a pop as his neck cracks, soreness from his sleepless nights. "I'm fine." Thomas looks skeptical but doesn't press on.

There's an entourage awaiting Luca when he finishes scrubbing at the end of the operation. Amber is at the head of the nursing station with a scowl on her face. Damien looks as if he's trying to pretend he doesn't want to be there and Holly is a little further back and looks like she was forced to tag along.

"This needs to end right now, Michaelson," Amber emphasizes every word intently.

"I don't know what you're talking about, Amber."

"You need to go talk to your sweetheart!" Damien bursts out. Everyone turns to him, shocked for his bluntness. "Look, it's not like you to be so torn up about a girl, man. I hate to admit but you've been looking like a lost puppy for the last week." Luca is shocked at Damien, never having seen him so serious. "Also, for all of our benefit, your moping has been fucking depressing."

Luca was just about to walk away until he hears someone clearing their throat. It's Holly coming forward.

"Please talk to her, okay?" Holly looks at Luca concerned. "The woman's a mess, acting like she doesn't care. For the last week, Bethany can barely look anyone in the eye. Every time she sees you she gets hopeful but is disappointed when she sees you're still avoiding her."

Luca clenches his fists and looks at all of his coworkers. "Thanks for all of your concerns, but I'd rather you didn't butt into my business."

A feeling of disappointment is heavy in the air as he walks away.

***

A new evening and Luca sighs for the third time in the past twenty minutes as he gazes down at a patient's chart. He's reread the same sentence over ten times, but the words just can't seem to stop blurring.

He's currently at the nursing station in the ER, a place where Bethany rarely comes down. It's become Luca's new hiding spot.

It's been a slow night. A few cooking accidents that ended in a trip to the ER and a few car accidents. But nothing out of the usual.

That's until a new patient stumbles through the doors.

The man is bloody. It's unclear whether it is his own, but there doesn't seem to be any running blood or open wounds. The man is tall and lanky, shaking like a leaf that will be blown away any minute. His eyes are dark and bloodshot red and he looks in a daze. Luca was about to stand up when he heard a voice nearby.

"Sir? Are you alright?"

Luca gets out of his chair quickly seeing Bethany standing in front of the stranger with both arms outstretched. "Sir, do you need any help?"

Then in slow motion, almost as if the man's snapping out of a daze, his head jerks up and eyes gazing on Bethany's. A split-second later, the man is charging in her direction causing Bethany to slam against the wall. The impact sent some triage kits to the ground.

The man's grip on Bethany tightens as he slams her up against the wall for a second time. Then, Bethany grabs for his arms but she's too slow. He tosses her to the ground and kicks her in the stomach. A second later, the crazy man's pinning Bethany down on the ground with his hands going for her throat.

The whimper slipping out of Bethany's mouth is what sends Luca into action. He sees red and nothing else matters except for his girlfriend.

He jumped on the deranged man, "Get off of

her!" and manages to grab the guy around the waist and pull him off her.

A minute later, hospital security came to the ER and Luca hands the crazy man off while pushing him away. Luca's hands flit over Bethany's groaning figure on the floor. His heart is racing.

"Bethany," his voice cracks as a few tears run down his cheeks. "Bethany, can you hear me?" A pained moan is the only answer he gets. From Luca's position on the floor, Luca yells to the hospital staff crowded behind him, "We need to get her into trauma! Move it, people!"

At his order, everyone snaps into motion. The next few minutes whiz by as the group works as a team to get Bethany into the trauma room and onto the table. She's hooked up to a heart monitor and her vitals are taken.

All Luca can see is the blood staining Bethany's coat and bruises blossoming sickly across her cheek. He's too shaken to check if the blood is Bethany's or the crazed madman's. It doesn't matter. All that matters is that Bethany is in pain.

Minutes later, Holly rushes inside. Her gaze flits

to Luca before her eyes stiffened and she's grabbing him by the hand. He's being dragged out of the door as there is panic as more doctors and surgeons arrive.

Bethany is hurt and they're taking him away. They're forcing him out and that's not right. Luca has to be there! His surgeon needs him now more than ever.

"Holly, stop! I need to be with her!" Luca is trying to pull away from her arms around him but suddenly, he feels so powerless. "Bethany needs me! Stop! Let me go! Holly!" Luca sees the head of hospital security, Officer Frank come and grab him from behind, leading him away from the scene.

Luca sits with his hands over his face as the man tries to calm him down. Officer Frank attempts to explain to Luca that Holly needs to go back and can't focus with Luca in the room.

"If anything fucking happens to her, it's on you all," Luca yells.

It really doesn't matter. None of Officer Frank's words matter to Luca at this very moment.

CHAPTER NINE

Luca is in an empty trauma room while Thomas is standing guard at the door trying to distract him and it isn't working.

"I'm sure she's fine!" Thomas smiles. "Holly should be here any minute now—"

As if summoned by some hidden freak of nature, Holly walks through the door with a clipboard. She looks exhausted, but there's not a sign of the look they always had when the doctors deliver bad news to the families.

Holly cuts right to the chase. "Bethany's fine." Her words caused Luca to let out an exhale; an invisible weight of gravity being lifted off his shoulders. "She's got some minor scrapes and bruising, along with some nasty internal bruising to her abdomen.

Her head cat scan showed no major issues, but she does have a concussion. We're going to keep her for a day or two for observation." Holly pauses as if she was debating her next set of words. "Bethany's very lucky you were there, Dr. Michaelson. That crazy guy would have killed her if it wasn't for your help."

Instead of asking to run off to Bethany's bedside as Thomas and Holly believes Luca will do, he sighs in relief and then turns to go rest in the on-call room.

Just because Bethany got hurt and Luca saved her life doesn't mean she doesn't want to see him. Luca wants nothing more than to make Bethany happy but still, he stays away.

A week later and he still hasn't seen her. He's taken his avoidance to another level, ducking into empty rooms and supply closets whenever he sees the brunette trauma surgeon coming his way. She appears to have recovered quickly, with only a few scrapes and bruises still visible.

But Bethany seems to be moodier than ever. On more than one occasion, Luca saw the trauma surgeon snapping at Holly and his other colleagues.

It's late on a Friday night and Luca is walking

down the hallways of the ICU with no real place to go in mind. Just when Luca's thoughts are wandering off to a certain trauma surgeon *again,* his pager goes off.

It's from trauma in OR three. Luca assumes it's Holly and huffs before taking off down the opposite end of the hallway.

When he comes inside the operating room masked, he finds the hospital staff is already cleaning up from an operation.

And Bethany is standing in the room's center as the only doctor on sight.

Luca does everything to keep his composure though his heart is racing faster than ever. "You paged?" He prays his voice doesn't crack.

Bethany crosses her arms and slightly grins. "Yes, I did." She chuckles but stops abruptly. "Since this seems to be the only way I'll be able to talk to you."

Luca tries to conceal his facial expression but fails when he sees Bethany's eyes harden.

"Doctor, listen—"

A burst of laughter comes from the trauma surgeon. "No! You do not get to avoid me for close to three weeks and then try and talk your way out of this! You're going to listen to me now whether you like it or not."

Luca steps back and raises his hands to show his peace. Bethany sighs before taking her scrub cap off and clutching it in her hands. "I wanted to thank you, for saving my life," her eyes are fixed on the ground. "I could have died that night. So, you know, I'm grateful for your assistance. Thanks."

Luca opens his mouth to speak but Bethany holds up a finger halting him. "I need you to tell me," she pauses for a second before looking straight into Luca's eyes while her gaze is piercing his soul. "I need you to tell me what you were saying that night with Damien, Amber, and Thoms," she demands, with no room for excuses.

Luca sighs and slumps back against the wall. "Bethany, I like you and all—"

He doesn't get far before he's being interrupted again. "I more than like you!" Bethany's words ripped Luca's heart out, causing his hands to thrust forward. "Damn it!" he curses and starts pacing back and forth.

The urge to tell her what he meant is stronger than ever. Bethany cares for him, probably more than Luca feels for her. Their relationship has been on pause over a huge misunderstanding. With Luca never feeling this way over a woman, damn it if he's not going to let this go now.

"You mean—" Lucas sighs and steels himself by walking forward a few steps. "You mean the world to me." Bethany's shocked look urges him on. "That night, I was trying to get advice from Thomas and ask about what to do next about us. Then I lied when Damien and Amber kept pressing me. I'm sorry." he gestures. "Still, we never once had a conversation about *what* we want in this relationship."

Bethany crosses her arms again. "Wasn't it obvious? Did I think you would want me for more than a quick fuck? Maybe. Luca, I heard about your other rendezvous and I'm not that kind of girl, you know. From the beginning, you never once said where we're going with this-"

"I didn't want you to hear that! Most of that nonsense isn't true." Luca's tone grows desperate not wanting to let Bethany continue to doubt him. "I never brought it up and was waiting for the right time to have a conversation about it."

Bethany still looks wary causing Luca to step forward and grab for one of her hands. The warmth of Bethany's palm in his is almost enough to stop him in his tracks but he has to reassure her. "You're the first person I've ever considered being in a relationship with. I'm almost thirty and have never felt for a person the way I feel about you. I don't know how to express that but with you, I'm willing to find out."

Bethany's mouth is hanging open in shock, her eyes twinkling with hope. She still hasn't let go of Luca's hand. "Bethany, you're the most wonderful person I've met, inside and out. You always put your patients' needs before your own, even when you don't need to. Don't ever doubt that you're the perfect soul for me."

Her grip tightens before speaking. "You're meaning to tell me that this was just a huge misunderstanding? That all you meant by that was that you needed to ask me first?"

Luca just nods as a lump suddenly forms in his throat at the wide smile Bethany shoots his way. A second passes before Bethany's fingers are twining into Luca's curly hair and he's being tugged forward.

Their lips slam together, weeks of desperation pouring out between them. Luca moans obscenely into Bethany's mouth as his tongue runs along her teeth. As Bethany sucks at Luca's bottom lip, he slips his hands to her ass and squeezes. The laugh he receives is lost in the moment.

They remain like this for minutes. The quietness of a weekday night in the OR. There is nothing else to disturb them as they wrapped around each other like a blanket.

Luca pulls away slightly. "So," he whispers. "Be my fiance?" he grins and Bethany can do nothing but chuckle pulling Luca in for another deep long kiss.

CHAPTER TEN

The next morning finds Luca hugging Bethany as the couple walks towards the nurse's station.

Thomas and Holly are resting behind the counter, the first of the two looking far too merry for the early hour. Amber is furiously writing in a chart, and all three of them seem to be disregarding Damien, who is gesturing wildly with a cocky smile on his face, no doubt spinning one of his unbelievable tales to one of nursing assistants.

Luca squeezes Bethany's hand as she nervously pushes her thick-rimmed glasses up her nose. It's amazing to see how comfortable the trauma surgeon can be and then turn immediately shy around others.

"Your attention everyone," Luca says after clearing his throat. The four surgeons look up at him, their eyes zeroing in on their clasped hands. "I would like to introduce you to someone," Luca says with a flourish as he tugs Bethany forward slightly. She's already blushing this early in the morning.

Amber's face shows confusion. "Luca, we already know—"

Luca interrupts her with an eye roll and his fingers tighten minutely around Bethany's. "Everyone, meet Bethany," he smirks quickly before continuing. "My fiance."

Bethany puts her hand over her mouth in shock. Luca hears Amber and Holly cheering and Thomas clapping. He can even hear Damien letting out a sigh of relief with a 'thank god' muttered.

Bethany continues smiling as she leans forward to give Luca a small peck. As she goes to pull away, Luca snakes a hand into her dark hair and opens his mouth. Bethany gasps in pleasure as they kiss, not giving a damn if they have an audience.

As they continue kissing, Luca can hear everyone's pagers go off. The four other surgeons scoff and laugh as they run off down the hall, leaving the two love-birds alone.

Bethany sighs and rests her forehead against Luca's. "I think they will need us," she says as she goes to reach for his pager. Luca stops her by grabbing her face and rubbing her cheeks.

"They can wait a few minutes," he says into the stillness between their lips. Bethany smiles as they bask in comfortable silence. "Hey, Beth?" Bethany hums and Luca takes a deep breath. "I love you."

Bethany looks a bit in shock and then her expression changes into one of total peace. "I love you too." They're already at the word 'love' and Luca doesn't have a problem with it. He knows what he feels for Bethany is a once-in-a-lifetime thing. He's sure they'll get married soon.

"Winstead! Michaelson! We need you in the ER!"

With that, Bethany gives Luca another quick peck before she's being pulled down the hallway, both of their game faces are on.

And they will be alright.